# TWO of a kind™ Diaries

**Look for more**

 ™

**titles:**

*#1 It's a Twin Thing*
*#2 How to Flunk Your First Date*
*#3 The Sleepover Secret*
*#4 One Twin Too Many*
*#5 To Snoop or Not to Snoop*
*#6 My Sister the Supermodel*
*#7 Two's a Crowd*
*#8 Let's Party*

# Calling All Boys

by Judy Katschke
from the series created by
**Robert Griffard & Howard Adler**

▦HarperEntertainment
*An Imprint of HarperCollinsPublishers*
**A PARACHUTE PRESS BOOK**

**A PARACHUTE PRESS BOOK**

Parachute Publishing, L.L.C.
156 Fifth Avenue, Suite 302
New York, NY 10010

Published by
HarperEntertainment
*An Imprint of* HarperCollins*Publishers*
10 East 53rd Street, New York, NY 10022-5299

TWO OF A KIND books created and produced by
Parachute Press, L.L.C., in cooperation with Dualstar Publications,
a division of Dualstar Entertainment Group, L.L.C.,
published by HarperEntertainment, an imprint of
HarperCollins *Publishers*.

For information address HarperCollins Publishers Inc.,
10 East 53rd Street, New York, NY 10022-5299.

ISBN 0-06-106579-X

First printing: February 2000

Printed in the United States of America

Visit HarperEntertainment on the World Wide Web at
www.harpercollins.com

10  9

# Chapter 1

# Monday

Dear Diary,

This is it! The last Monday in January  and the first day of my new life. Well, for the next five months anyway.

Everything happened so fast! You see, my twin sister Mary-Kate and I thought we'd be going to White Oak Academy for Girls next fall. I was totally psyched about crunching my way to class through all those red and yellow New Hampshire leaves. But when Dad told us we'd be starting this *January* instead—I almost flipped!

"Can you imagine living in a real dormitory?" I asked my sister in the car. "I never slept in school before."

"Oh, yes, you did," Mary-Kate said. "Just last month you dozed off during that boring movie in assembly. You drooled all over my shoulder!"

Okay, I admit that I dozed off during the Wonders of Bull Seals. But I *never* drool!

Mary-Kate and I did our share of dozing right here

 in the car. That's because Dad's been driving for almost two days now.

Dad just let out a big sigh. I know what he's thinking—that he's going to miss us.

But he was about to have his own adventure. You see, Diary, the reason Mary-Kate and I are going away to boarding school in the first place is because Dad is going to the Amazon rain forest.

Amazing! When it comes to research, our dad, Professor Kevin Burke, never goes farther than the library or the Internet. And the closest he's ever come to a rain forest is the Jungle Cruise at Disney World!

Now Dad's going halfway around the world to study—get this—how many different species of insects exist in one single tree!!

"You're going to go all the way to South America to count *bugs*?" I said when he explained his assignment.

"Sure," Dad said. "Where else am I going to find so many different species of exotic insects?"

"Under our kitchen sink!" Mary-Kate said.

"Okay, okay," Dad said with a grin. "It's an icky job but somebody's got to do it. And the university chose me. It's quite an honor, you know."

# Calling All Boys

We knew. We also knew who Dad would take along as his student intern—Carrie! Carrie is our baby-sitter but she does a lot more than sit. She listens to cool music and always has great advice on just about everything. She also has the best clothes.

"You don't know what you're in for, Carrie," I told her just two days ago. "There probably isn't a mall within ten miles of the Amazon jungle. How will you survive?"

She just smiled at me and said, "Catalogs?"

Let's face it. The real question is—how will Mary-Kate and I survive without Carrie? We tell her practically everything. But leave it to Carrie to read our minds and give us the perfect good-bye present. Stationery—so we can keep in touch with her!

Dad gave us the perfect presents too—diaries! So Mary-Kate and I can be in touch with our feelings.

I'll be doing a lot of that! Because so far my feelings have been everything from ecstatic to scared. That's right—scared. And in case you're wondering what I'm scared about, here's a list:

1) What if Mary-Kate and I never fit in? 2) What if I don't see one single boy for the next five months? 3) And what if my friends in Chicago don't even know that I'm gone? (I added that one last week after Jennifer and Nicole treated me to a farewell

3

pizza with spinach and cheese.)

Here's how that scene went: "I'm going to eat five slices," I told them. "One for every month I'm going to be away." (Okay, I only made it to two slices.)

When we were finished pigging out, Jennifer turned to Nicole. "Are you going to Akilah's sleep-over on Saturday night?" she asked.

"Wouldn't miss it," Nicole said through a mouth-ful of mozzarella. "I heard that Akilah just got a big-screen TV."

So I chimed in: "Cool! I'll bring my new DVD's."

Silence. I looked up and saw Jennifer and Nicole staring at me.

"What?" I asked. "Do I have spinach stuck in my teeth?"

"Ashley, have you forgotten something?" Jennifer asked.

"You're not going to be here on Saturday," Nicole said. "In fact, you won't be here for the next . . . twenty Saturdays!"

Twenty Saturdays! That's tons of ballet lessons, sleepovers, and movies that are going to happen without me! And what if nobody even notices?

I better start making lots of

4

new friends right away. I don't want to be thinking about all of the parties I'm missing—I want to think about all of the parties I'm *throwing*!

Are we there yet??


Dear Diary,

If my handwriting seems a little squiggly it's not me—it's the bumps in the road. And if it takes me awhile to get used to writing in a diary, it's because I never had one before. Ashley was always the one with a diary. I was always the one trying to read it.

I wasn't even going to start writing until I got to school, but I've got to do something. Dad has been listening to golden oldies on the car radio for almost an hour and I packed my Walkman in my trunk.

Notice how I say 'trunk' as in singular. Ashley packed two whole trunks—plus a backpack—plus a suitcase!

Her comment two days ago: "Of course I'm packing all of my clothes." She was digging through her closet like an archeologist. "You never know when I might need them."

So I said, "Like your toe shoes?" I picked them up and waved them in the air.

Ashley rolled her eyes so far back in her head

that I bet she could see her own brain. She grabbed the shoes back. "Mary-Kate, White Oak has a whole performing arts center—with stadium seating," she said. I guess she's planning on making a few appearances there.

As for me, I made sure I packed my softball, my glove, even my bat. White Oak Academy has a killer team.

Last summer, Dad, Ashley, and I drove to the  school for a visit. The first person who met us there was Mrs. Prichard, the "headmistress." She showed us around the school and told us all about it, including how great the athletic department is.

Still, it was really hard to say good-bye to my two friends and softball teammates, Max and Brian.

"We might as well face it right now, Mary-Kate," Max said yesterday. He shook his head as we sat on the stoop. "Without you at the bat, the Belmont Bashers are history!"

"Wow, guys," I told Max and Brian. "Does that mean you're going to miss me?"

"Are you kidding?" Max said. He heaved a big sigh. "I don't want to get sappy, but this block won't be the same without you. Right, Brian?"

"You bet!" Brian said, nodding.

I was starting to feel all warm and fuzzy when Brian turned to me with wide eyes.

"Mary-Kate?" he asked. "If you're not taking your skateboard, can I borrow it?"

"And don't worry about your *Sports Illustrated* subscription," Max suggested. He patted my shoulder. "You can forward it to me."

So much for sappy good-byes!

Honestly, I'm worried about making the White Oak team. What if I'm not good enough? I could cut it on the Bashers, but let's face it—Max and Brian are hardly Mark McGwire and Sammy Sosa.

I'm also worried about not having my math tutor, Taylor Donovan, around to help me with my homework and to study for tests. I mean, what if this new school teaches space-age math? And what if they don't allow calculators? I'm doomed!

"We're almost there!" Dad just called back over the front seat. I hate it when he does that, because he always takes his eyes off the road and I think he's going to drive off into a ditch.

"Keep your eyes peeled for the school," Dad said over his shoulder. "Do you remember what it looks like?"

"We remember, Dad! Just keep driving," I said.

The White Oak Academy for Girls is the most awesome school I ever saw. For one thing, it's not just one building like our school in Chicago. There's a separate building for the library, the computer center, the performing arts center—even a whole building just for *math*.

The dorms, or "houses," as White Oak calls them, are all lined up on one long street. And there are trees all over the place. No wonder they call it White Oak!

But the coolest sight is the Main Building. It's made of gray stone with ivy crawling all over the walls in the summer. It has two tall towers and stone gargoyles peering down from just about every-where!

"It's not a school—it's a castle!" I said.

"Yeah!" Ashley said and sighed. "Now all it needs is a handsome prince!"

"Or a fire-breathing dragon!" I joked.

But Ashley has a point. This whole boarding school adventure is sort of like a fairy tale.

Whoops, got to go. Ashley just had a White Oak sighting.

Oh, and by the way. I think I'm going to get used to this diary deal. Over and out!

Dear Diary,

You will never guess in a gazillion  years where Mary-Kate and I are right now. Give up? *The student lounge*! In Chicago the only ones who had a lounge were the teachers!

The White Oak Academy is exactly the way I remembered it. Except today it's filled with girls—*and* one of the cutest boys I ever saw! I was totally psyched until I pointed him out to Mary-Kate.

"Reality check! Reality check!" Mary-Kate announced in my ear. "This is a *girls'* school, remember?"

"Oh, yeah," I said as it hit me. Then I smiled. "But somebody here has a really cute brother!"

Mrs. Prichard was exactly the way I remembered her, too. She was dressed in a gray wool dress with a white collar. Her silver hair was short and she wore glasses studded with rhine-stones on a chain around her neck.

"I think you girls are going to like The White Oak Academy," Mrs. Prichard said from behind her desk.

Mary-Kate and I smiled at each other.

We already *knew* we were!

"Mary-Kate and Ashley have a cousin who goes to The Harrington School for Boys," Dad went on. "His name is Jeremy Burke."

Mrs. Prichard nodded. The Harrington School is right down the road.

"Then you'll be happy to know that the White Oak Academy and the Harrington School meet together each week for classes," Mrs. Prichard said. She tilted her glasses as she looked at a paper on her desk. "You'll be joining the boys for history on Tuesdays and lab every other Monday."

"Boys?" I pumped my fist in the air. "Ye-es!"

Mrs. Prichard looked at me over her glasses.

"I mean . . . yes, that's good to know," I said quickly.

As Mrs. Prichard spoke I realized what a different world boarding school would be. Like, the seventh grade isn't called the seventh grade—it's called First Form. There's a special study period and a curfew, which means all of us go to bed at the same time.

"And there's hearty hot oatmeal for breakfast every morning," Mrs. Prichard added with a smile. "It's been a tradition at White Oak since 1895."

*Yummy since 1895*

**10**

I just hope they aren't serving the *same* oatmeal from 1895.

Then Mrs. Prichard handed Mary-Kate and me our gym suits and our schedules. We have three classes together—English, science lab, and history. That's cool!

"Now, girls," Mrs. Prichard said with a smile. "After I direct your father to the business office, I'll show you the student lounge. I think you'll be pleasantly surprised."

Mrs. Prichard wasn't kidding! The first thing Mary-Kate and I saw when we walked in there were video games, a few Ping-Pong tables, a CD player, and big cushy chairs. There was even a fish tank and a whole row of snack machines.

Two teenage girls sat at a table playing chess. Two more were hitting a Ping-Pong ball back and forth. Another girl with long black hair was tapping on the fish tank and making fish faces.

I took a deep breath. This was the moment I had been waiting for. Now was the perfect opportunity to start making friends at White Oak. But how should I do it? Should I just go up and introduce myself?

Of course, Mary-Kate headed straight for the video games. "Cool! *Alien Morons from Mars*—my favorite!"

I guess Mary-Kate wasn't worried about *her* social life.

Maybe food would help me find the courage to talk to someone. I made a beeline to the snack machine for a grape fruit roll-up. I was just about to tear it open when the girl with dark hair walked over.

"Hi," she said. "I'm Wendy Linden."

"Ashley Burke," I said, smiling. "Are you in the seventh grade too?"

Wendy chuckled. "You mean First Form?"

"Du-uh!" I gave my forehead a little whack. "What do they call teachers around here?"

Wendy smiled. "Teachers."

"Good!" I sighed.

After saying a quick "hi" to Mary-Kate, Wendy challenged me to a fierce game of Ping-Pong. I stashed my fruit roll-up in my pocket and grabbed a paddle.

While Wendy and I whacked the little ball back and forth she clued me in on the school. She reminded me that everyone on a floor shares *one* bathroom. *That* does not thrill me. I mean, what if someone washes their feet in the sink? Or spits on the faucet while they brush their teeth?

"You'll get over it," Wendy said. She gave the ball a slug. "And if anybody gets too gross, just bring it to the head."

I wrinkled my nose. "*Whose* head?"

Wendy began to giggle. "The *headmistress*—Mrs. Prichard!"

I felt myself blush. Another White Oak blooper!

"And check this out," Wendy said, bouncing the Ping-Pong ball on the table. "At the end of the school year Mrs. Prichard invites the girls with the best grades to *tea*."

"Tea?" I asked. "The only time I drink tea is when I have the flu."

The door opened and two girls walked in. One had short blond hair and was wearing a fleece shirt and jeans. The other girl had brown layered hair and big green eyes. She was dressed in black corduroy pants and a light blue sweater, which, if I'm not mistaken, was cashmere!

As the two girls headed for the snack machine, Wendy came around the table and whispered:

"The one in the blue sweater is Dana Woletsky— the Queen of First Form," Wendy explained. "She throws all the best parties. But if she doesn't like you, stay out of her way."

"Who's the other girl?" I asked.

"Kristen Lindquist," Wendy said. "One of Dana's gazillion friends."

That's when it hit me—if I could get in with this Dana Woletsky and her friends, fitting in at White Oak would be a piece of cake!

*Piece of ← cake!*

I put down my Ping-Pong paddle and watched Dana. Her hands were on her hips as she stared at the snack machine. "Okay," she said, turning around. "Who took the last fruit roll-up?"

Whoops! Okay, so that wasn't the conversation opener I was looking for. I shoved my grape fruit roll-up deeper into my pocket.

Dana grumbled a bit, then finally settled for chocolate-covered raisins. Then she and Kristin left the student lounge and I got to work.

"Wendy," I said. "You have to introduce me to Dana. As soon as possible."

"Are you serious?" she cried. "You'd have a better chance chumming up with Mrs. Prichard. Besides, I hardly know Dana."

I shrugged. I'll just have to introduce myself, then.

When the Ping-Pong game was over (I won!), Wendy and I sat down on a big purple couch to compare schedules.

# Calling All Boys

"Way cool!" Wendy said. "You're in my English class!"

"I love English," I told Wendy. "It's always been my favorite subject."

Wendy looked skeptical. "Oh, yeah?" she asked. "I guess you haven't met Ms. Bloomberg yet."

"Ms. Bloomberg—is that our teacher?" I asked excitedly. "What's she like? Is she nice?"

"Um," Wendy said, standing up. "I have to go to my room now. I forgot to . . . water my Chia Pet."

I watched Wendy leave the Student Lounge. She was nice but she sure acted strange when she mentioned Ms. Bloomberg. Whatever. Maybe English isn't her best subject.

I leaned back on the cushy purple couch. I was about to put my feet up but I stopped in mid-air. Dad hates it when Mary-Kate and I put our sneakers on the couch.

Dad . . . ?

Hey, wait a minute—Dad won't be here to tell me to take my feet off the couch. Or to do my homework. Or to put the cap back on the toothpaste tube. In fact—he won't even be around to say goodnight!

All of sudden, I felt my first small pang of homesickness. Not really a pang—more like a ping.

But when I saw Mary-Kate by the video games I

felt better. With my twin sister as my roommate, this school ought to feel something like home. As long as her side of the room is still a mess!

Oh, well. It's a good thing I didn't have my feet on the couch because Dad just walked in. I'll catch you later, Diary. When Mary-Kate and I are settled in our *new room*!

Dear Diary,

News flash: Mary-Kate and I will *not* be sharing a room here at the White Oak school!!

"Sisters never share a room here," Mrs. Prichard told us today. "It's all part of White Oak Academy tradition."

In case you haven't already noticed, Diary, tradition here rules. But then Mrs. Prichard told us the reason for the split—"We want everyone to develop their own interests and make new friends." That makes sense to me—I guess.

Mrs. Prichard said that at least we'll be in the same house—Porter House—with about thirty other First Form girls. (The name of the other First Form house is Phipps.) But I've almost never slept without Mary-Kate in the room, and knowing that she might be all the way on some other floor made it even harder to say good-bye to Dad . . .

"Okay, girls," Dad said. He looked at his watch and took a long, deep breath. "I guess this is it." He held out his arms and gave each of us a big hug.

"Bye, Dad," I sniffed as he took a few steps back. "Have fun saving the rain forest."

"Just one more thing," Dad said. He reached into his bag. "I brought a little present for both of you. Something that will come in very handy."

Then right before our very eyes Dad pulled out—are you ready, Diary?—a cell phone! I couldn't believe it! The only kid I know with a cell phone is Jennifer Dilber. She uses her cell phone so much that—well, you've heard of hat-hair? Jennifer has phone-hair!

*Jennifer with phone hair*

"Are you sure this is for us?" Mary-Kate asked.

"Sure I'm sure," Dad said. He handed the phone to me. "Unless you know any other twins who are going away to school for five whole months."

There was no time to waste. I began punching in Jennifer's number. I mean, I had to tell someone the good news, right?

Wrong! Dad told us in his most serious Dad-voice that the phone is absolutely to be used for emergencies only. What a bummer.

"I'll be carrying my phone wherever I go so you can reach me any time," Dad explained.

The thought of Dad having a cell phone in the jungle blew me away. I mean, Tarzan should be so cool!

Then the fun was over and it was really time for Dad to leave. As he walked down the hall, Mary-Kate and I waved good-bye. We were still waving after Dad left the building.

*Tarzan Dad*

"Hello, Mary-Kate, hello, Ashley," a voice said.

Mary-Kate and I whirled around. A woman with blond hair stood behind us.

"I'm Miss Viola, the housemother," she explained. Miss Viola shook our hands. Then she told us (in a nice way) that cell phones aren't encouraged at White Oak.

Another tradition, I guess.

"Now, how would you like to meet your new roommates?" Miss Viola asked. "I'm sure they want to meet you."

I felt a shiver of excitement. My new life at the White Oak Academy was about to begin!

Mary-Kate and I pulled on our jackets and followed Miss Viola to Porter House. It's a huge old white house with green shutters and a big comfy lounge on the main floor. I wonder if we'll ever get to toast marshmallows in the fireplace?

Miss Viola brought me to my room first: Number 25 on the third floor.

"I'm in Room 25," I pictured myself saying. "You know. The one with all the pizza parties and late night chats?"

After saying good-bye to Mary-Kate and wishing her luck, I grabbed the handle and opened the door.

"Hello?" I said, stepping inside. "Anybody home?"

No one answered. I looked around the room. The windows had strings of beads instead of curtains. One bed was covered with an Indian-print bedspread and a pile of pillows.

There were posters on the walls. But they weren't of celebrities—they were of William Shakespeare and this depressed-looking lady with her hair in a bun!

Depressed-looking lady (not Phoebe)

"Where am I?" I whispered to myself. A girl with curly brown hair and blue-rimmed glasses peeked out from behind a wicker screen. "Hi," she said softly. "I'm Phoebe Cahill. I guess we're roommates."

"I'm Ashley Burke." I walked around the screen and gave a little wave. Phoebe was sitting at a desk reading a book. I could see the title on the cover: *Romeo and Juliet*!

"*Romeo and Juliet*!" I said with a sigh. "Did you see the movie with Claire Danes and Leonardo DiCaprio? It was awesome!"

Phoebe blinked a couple of times behind her glasses. "If you say so," she said with a little shrug.

I sat down on my unmade bed and waited for my trunk to arrive. Phoebe didn't seem like the chatty type so I tried to break the ice. Chip by chip.

"I hope there's a decent mall around here," I said, figuring that clothes are always a good icebreaker, right? Wrong!

"Oh, I don't shop at malls," Phoebe said. "I buy all my clothes at vintage shops."

Vintage?

Phoebe ran to our closet and started pulling things out. She held up a pair of bell-bottom pants.

"These pants are from 1970!" Phoebe said excitedly. Then she picked up a pair of brown suede hip boots. "And these were worn by a real 1960's flower child!"

"I have a blue lava lamp at home," I said, trying to be cool. "It belonged to a real 70's disco king. My dad."

That warmed Phoebe right up, and she started telling me all about herself. She likes to write poetry. She explained that the woman in the poster is Emily Dickinson—the greatest poet in women's history and her personal hero.

Not only does Phoebe write poetry but she's an editor of the Lower School paper. Not too shabby.

I could tell Phoebe was trying to act interested when I started talking about my friends and my favorite rock groups. But I think it was hard for her to connect with what I was saying. Like she actually thought 'N Sync was a drain cleaner!

"I really should go back to my book," Phoebe said politely. "Romeo was about to take the poison."

"Sure," I said as Phoebe slipped back behind the screen. "I'll just start unpacking."

Okay, Phoebe Cahill is nice, even though she's not exactly what I expected. But I guess there'll be *lots* of surprises for me and Mary-Kate from now on!

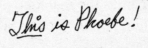

*This is Phoebe!*

# Chapter 2

# Tuesday

Dear Diary,

I did it!!! I didn't think I could do it, but I, Mary-Kate Burke, survived my first night at The White Oak Academy.

The first few hours were a little touch and go. When I heard that Ashley and I weren't going to be roommates, I felt like chasing Dad all the way to the

Amazon—snakes or no snakes. But when I stepped into Room Number 12 on the second floor, I knew things were going to be cool.

Why the sudden change? Picture this.

The first thing I saw were shelves full of sports trophies! And posters on the wall of Derek Jeter and Sammy Sosa.

Was I in my new room—or in heaven?

Then my roommate Campbell Smith walked in. She has short brown hair and brown eyes. And I knew she was an athlete by the way she shook my hand—a real bone-crusher!

Here comes the real kick—Campbell told me she was a pitcher on the Lower School softball team, the Mighty Oaks!

# Calling All Boys

When I told her that I played softball back in Chicago, she told me that maybe I could play on their team. All I had to do was pass the try-outs. Maybe Campbell will practice with me—it can't hurt having her as a roommate.

Of course, I did miss Ashley last night. It was weird having a strange girl sleeping in the next bed. Especially when she snores like a buzz saw!

Believe me, I was very happy to see Ashley first thing at breakfast. While we ate our oatmeal she told me all about her new roommate, Phoebe, and her funky clothes.

*my new roomie*

The oatmeal was better than I expected. But it's going to take awhile to get used to eating *three* meals *in school*. And last night at dinner I made the mistake of calling the room we ate in "the cafeteria." Boy, did everyone get a kick out of that!

"It's the *dining hall*!" Wendy said.

Wendy had a point. That room didn't look like any school cafeteria I'd ever seen. The floors were made of dark polished wood. So were the walls, which were covered with old portraits of women. Ashley guessed they were past headmistresses. I swore they were past cafeteria ladies without their hair nets. Whoops—I mean, dining hall ladies. As for the gargoyles on the ceiling, they're way cool. Even though they looked like they were about to swoop down any minute and grab our fried chicken!

*hungry gargoyle*

After breakfast, Ashley and I walked over to Morning Announcements. That's when everyone piles into the performing arts auditorium to yawn and listen to what Mrs. Prichard has to tell us.

Ashley was just beginning to tell me about Dana what's-her-name when Mrs. Prichard walked out on stage.

"Good morning, girls," Mrs. Prichard said. "I'd like to welcome you back from winter break. Why don't we start our new semester by greeting our two newest White Oak girls, Mary-Kate and Ashley Burke?"

Ashley jumped up and started waving like a movie star. I just nodded and smiled.

*Ashley waving at her fans*

After talking about the new school computers and gym suits, Mrs. Prichard looked really excited. "Girls, February is almost here and you know what that means!" she said with a grin. "Next week is our annual Sadie Hawkins Day Dance with the Harrington School for Boys."

Mrs. Prichard gave us all a few seconds to whisper and get excited. Ashley looked practically ecstatic.

"A dance?" Ashley gasped. "You mean with a DJ?"

A girl in front of us turned around. "It's a square dance," she whispered. "You know—do-si-do and swing your partner—that kind of stuff."

Ashley looked horrified. "A square dance?" she groaned. "Cor-ny!"

*Corn Dancing*

But then Mrs. Prichard said the magic words.

"As you know," she said, "it's a tradition that the girls ask the boys to the Sadie Hawkins Day Dance."

Everyone let out this ear-splitting cheer.

"Now that's my kind of square dance," Ashley declared. "Bring on the fiddles!"

The Sadie Hawkins Day Dance might be square, but it could be fun. But there was one problem. A *major* problem . . .

"Ashley?" I whispered. "I don't want to burst your bubble. But how are we going to ask out boys when we don't know any?"

Ashley sunk into her seat. "You're right," she said. "I never thought of that!"

The thought stayed with us as we walked to English class.

"There's only one guy we know at Harrington," I sighed, clutching my books. "And that's *Jeremy*."

Ashley grabbed my arm. "Mary-Kate, that's it!" she said. "I just figured out how we can meet guys at Harrington. We can ask Jeremy to help us."

"Jeremy—the family clown?" I cried. "Ashley, have you forgotten those whoopie cushions he laid out last Thanksgiving? Or those wind-up chattering teeth he gave Grandma for her seventieth birthday?"

"Okay, so he likes a good laugh now and then," Ashley said. "But I know this will work. In fact, I'm going to give Jeremy a call as soon as possible."

"Call?" I asked. "As in—with the cell phone?"

Ashley just smiled.

"Nice try, Ashley," I told her. "But you remember what Dad said. We can only use that phone in an emergency."

Ashley pulled me aside. She had that determined look in her eye that I knew so well.

"Mary-Kate," she whispered. "This *is* an emergency!"

# Calling All Boys

I should have known!

When it comes to boys, nothing stops my sister!

Dear Diary,

I've got good news and bad news. First, let's get the bad news out of the way . . .

There I was in my new English class this morning. Sitting behind my desk with my notebooks stacked neatly. All set to impress my new English teacher, Ms. Bloomberg.

So when she passed out the reading list for the semester I studied it very carefully.

"*Treasure Island, The Diary of Anne Frank, Oliver Twist,*" I read under my breath. "*Oliver Twist?*"

My hand shot up.

"Yes, Ashley?" Ms. Bloomberg asked.

"Ms. Bloomberg, I see that *Oliver Twist* is on the reading list," I said. "I already read *Oliver Twist* back in Chicago."

Ms. Bloomberg cocked an eyebrow. "And you're telling me this because?"

I shrugged. "May I read another book instead?"

The class went dead silent. We're talking soundproof booth. I could see Wendy shaking her head. What did I say?

"Ashley," Ms. Bloomberg said. "What you learned back in Chicago has nothing to do with what you learn in my class."

"Yes, Ms. Bloomberg, but—" I started to say.

Ms. Bloomberg folded her arms across her chest. "And since you know so much about *Oliver Twist*," she went on, "perhaps you'd like to tell us what you thought about it."

"Thought about it?" I repeated.

"In addition to reading *Treasure Island* with the rest of the students this week," Ms. Bloomberg said, "I'd like you to re-read *Oliver Twist* and write a five-page report which you will read to the class next Thursday."

My blood froze. "B-but," I stammered. "Won't I be giving away the . . . ending?"

"Next Thursday," Ms. Bloomberg repeated.

Thursday! That was less than two weeks away! How was I going to read two books *and* write a report *and* do all my other homework?

What could I say? I just went with, "Yes, Ms. Bloomberg," and sat down. I felt a humongous lump in my throat—I think it was my foot!!

But enough about that. Ready for some good news? My little plan for the

# Calling All Boys

Sadie Hawkins Day dance worked. Right after history class Mary-Kate and I sneaked into the girls' room and pulled out our cell phone. Luckily the First Form boys were on their break so Jeremy was in his house.

"Hey, cuz!" Jeremy said when he answered. "What's up?"

Mary-Kate was leaning hard on my shoulder trying to listen in. Ouch!

"Jeremy, we need your help," I told him. "The Sadie Hawkins Day Dance is coming up and Mary-Kate and I don't know any boys at Harrington. Besides you."

"So?" Jeremy asked. Naturally, he wasn't going to make this easy for me. He was like the brother I never had—or wanted.

"So we want you to help us," I said. "You know, give us the names of some guys that Mary-Kate and I might like."

"Oh, I get it," Jeremy laughed. "You want me to be the *looooove* connection!"

I held the phone away from my ear while Jeremy made loud kissing noises. Why did I think this was a good idea again?

"Come on, Jeremy, it shouldn't be hard," I said firmly. "You know the type of guy I like."

"Yeah, *all* of them!" Jeremy joked. "Okay, okay. Give me a second to think."

I held my breath as Jeremy thought. Mary-Kate hummed the *Jeopardy!* theme song.

"No problemo!" Jeremy finally said. "I know just the guys for both of you."

"Who?" I asked excitedly.

Jeremy suggested a First Form guy named P.J. for Mary-Kate. "P.J. is a lot like your sister," he said. "Trophies on his shelf, that kind of thing."

"His name is P.J." I whispered to Mary-Kate. "He's an *athlete!*"

My sister gave me a thumbs-up sign.

"What about me?" I asked Jeremy.

"Oh, you and Ross Lambert would really hit it off," Jeremy said. "He's a straight 'A' First Form student and captain of the debating team. And during winter and summer breaks, he models."

"A model!" I squealed. I pictured a god in khakis and a fleece vest.

"Jeremy?" I asked. "Were Ross and P.J. in our history class today? Second period?"

"No," Jeremy said. "They have history tomorrow with me. But they have science lab next Monday at two

*Ross Lambert*

in the afternoon. Are you in our class, too?"

"Yup," I said. "Then that's when we'll ask them to the dance."

"Um—I wouldn't wait that long if I were you," Jeremy said. "Those guys are pretty hot stuff!"

"Okay, then we'll call them on our cell phone," I said. I could hear Mary-Kate groaning over my shoulder.

"Now you're talking," Jeremy said. "Ross is in Webb House, same as me. P.J. is in Vickers. Call them tomorrow around two o'clock. That's when we go to our rooms to exchange our books."

"Make it snappy, Ashley," Mary-Kate said, shaking my arm. "Someone's coming."

"Thanks, Jeremy," I said. "Got to go. Bye." I clicked off the phone and gave my sister's arm a squeeze.

"It worked, Mary-Kate," I said.

Mary-Kate nodded. "All systems go!"

Diary, is this awesome or what? Now all Mary-Kate and I have to do is call these guys and get dates for the Sadie Hawkins Day Dance.

But until then, I have a date with *Oliver Twist*!

# Chapter 3

# Wednesday

Dear Diary,

Sorry I can't write tonight, Diary. There's open batting practice in the gym for everyone, and I've got to get back in the swing. See ya!

Dear Diary,

I know, I know. I should be re-reading *Oliver Twist* right now but I have so much to tell you.

It started when we all went outside for midday break. The track field in the back of the school was completely covered with snow.

We were walking around making footprints in the snow when Wendy had an idea.

"Why don't we build snowmen?" Wendy asked.

Phoebe cleared her throat. "You mean snow *people*!" she corrected. "We have to stand up for equality for women!"

"She does have a point," I whispered to Mary-Kate.

"Yeah, but Frosty the Snowperson just doesn't cut it," Mary-Kate whispered back.

With everyone busy building snow people and

Frosty the Snowperson

having snowball fights, it was the perfect time for Mary-Kate and me to call our dates. It was 2:00—just the time Jeremy told us to call.

Using a White Oak/Harrington phone sheet I took from the main office, I dialed Ross Lambert's house number. I couldn't tell whether my hands were shaking from the cold or from the excitement. It took a few minutes for Ross's roommate to track him down, but finally Ross came to the phone!

"Hi, Ross," I said. "This is Ashley Burke. You know, Jeremy's cousin?"

"I know who you are," Ross said. "Jeremy told me you were going to call. He even showed me your picture. The one where you're holding that big fish you caught. You looked totally cute!"

*Cute*—he thought I was cute!

Okay, so it was a picture of Mary-Kate, but everyone says we look identical.

"Thanks!" I said.

Mary-Kate wiggled my arm.

"Cut to the chase!" she whispered. "Cut to the chase!"

"Ross, the Sadie Hawkins Day Dance is next week," I said, trying to sound cool. "Would you like to go with me?"

"Sure," Ross said.

"Bingo!" I cheered. Then I felt myself blush. "I mean . . . it should be a lot more fun than—bingo!"

We made our plans, said good-bye, and hung up.

"I'm in love, I'm in love!" I swooned, spinning around in the snow.

"In love?" Mary-Kate cried. "But you haven't even met the guy yet!"

"I don't have to," I said. "I can tell by Ross's warm and caring voice that we're perfect soul-mates."

"And being a male model doesn't hurt either," Mary-Kate added.

"Of course not," I said, holding the cell phone out to Mary-Kate. "Your turn."

But Mary-Kate just stared at the phone.

"What's the matter?" I asked.

"Ashley, this sort of stuff doesn't come easy for me!" Mary-Kate said. "The only time I ever call boys is to arrange softball games. You know that!"

"So pretend you and P.J. are going to a Cubs

game," I said, thrusting the phone forward. "Go on."

"Okay, okay," Mary-Kate muttered. She dialed P.J.'s number and waited.

"Hello?" Mary-Kate said. "Is P.J. around? . . . He's what? . . . He's playing the *organ*?"

I bit my lip. Electric guitars are cool. So are drums and saxophones. But organs? No way! I wondered what my sister thought of that. I couldn't read Mary-Kate's expression.

It took awhile for P.J. to come to the phone. But when he did, Mary-Kate got right down to business.

"Okay, P.J., I don't know you and you don't know me," Mary-Kate said. "But I need a date for the Cubs Game—I mean—the Sadie Hawkins Day Dance next week. How about it?"

Mary-Kate waited a few seconds. Then she gave me a thumbs-up sign and made the date.

"You see? It worked!" I said after Mary-Kate switched off the phone. "But what's this about him playing the organ? Aren't organs kind of . . . unusual?"

"Not if you're at a baseball stadium," Mary-Kate said, her eyes shining.

Why didn't I think of that?

"We did it!" I exclaimed as I gave Mary-Kate a

big high-five. "We got dates for the Sadie Hawkins Day Dance!"

"Way to go!" Mary-Kate cheered.

"Now, remember," I told my sister. "This whole thing about Jeremy and the cell phone will be our little secret."

"Did I just hear right?" Wendy asked, peeking out from behind her snowman. "You two got dates? Just like that?"

Mary-Kate and I looked at each other. So much for little secrets!

I took a deep breath and told Wendy all about our cell phone and our cousin at the Harrington School for Boys.

"You are soooo lucky," Wendy said. "I still can't get up the nerve to ask out Tyler."

"Tyler?" I repeated.

"Tyler Kelliher, the lead clarinetist in the Harrington band," Wendy explained. "I once found his reed under his chair. I've been sleeping with it under my pillow for months."

"That is so gross!" Mary-Kate cried.

"No, it's not," I sighed. "It's true love." It was then that I had the most fantastic idea!

"Wendy?" I asked. "How would you like us to

use our cell phone to call Tyler?"

"You mean ask him out for me?" Wendy whispered. Her eyes were wide open. "You'd really do that?"

Mary-Kate dragged me aside. "Earth to Ashley," she whispered. "We're not allowed to use our cell phone, remember?"

I remembered. But I also remembered how nice Wendy was to me on my first day in the Student Lounge.

"Just this once, Mary-Kate," I promised.

Just this once. Lucky I didn't put it in writing. Because later at dinner who should approach us at the frozen yogurt machine but Dana Woletsky!

"Ashley? Mary-Kate?" Dana asked. She looked at us as she sprinkled carob chips over her strawberry yogurt. "I hear you two have a cell phone."

Wow—I couldn't believe it! Dana Woletsky actually knows our names—and she was talking to us. But why? Was she going to blow the whistle on our cell phone? Far from it.

"Some of my friends need dates for the Sadie Hawkins Day Dance," Dana said. "Can you fix them up with some boys at Harrington?"

Did I just hear right? Was the coolest girl in school asking Mary-Kate and me for a favor?

"No problem," I said quickly.

"Wait a minute, wait a minute," Mary-Kate told me. She turned to Dana. "You and your friends aren't new here like Ashley and I are. Why would you need help meeting boys?"

"We only started in September," Dana explained. "That's not enough time to get to know boys. Besides, some girls like boys they don't have classes with. Like Second Form boys they've seen in town."

"Dana, say no more!" I said with a grin. "Mary-Kate and I will be glad to help out."

I could hear Mary-Kate making little gasping noises.

"Cool," Dana said. "I'll give you a list of my friends and the boys they like."

"How about you, Dana?" I asked.

"Oh, don't bother," Dana said. She picked up her tray and began walking away. "I already have a boyfriend at Harrington. He knows he's going with me."

"Are you nuts?" Mary-Kate cried after Dana walked to her table. "You heard what Dad and Miss Viola said. And what is this—a dating service?"

My sister just didn't have a clue. "May I remind you that Dana Woletsky is the coolest First Form girl at White Oak?" I said. "And that this is a great chance to make friends?"

"But, Ashley—" Mary-Kate started, but I cut her off.

"It's not a dating service." I tilted my head and tapped my chin.

"Consider it . . . a Friendship Service!"

# Chapter 4

# Friday

Dear Diary,

Diary, our friendship service has taken off. It's only been two days and already we fixed up six of Dana's friends. One was so grateful she gave me a gift!

"What's this?" I asked Kristin Lindquist as she handed me a pink plastic bottle.

"It's strawberry glitter body lotion," Kristin said. "It actually makes you glow in the dark."

"Super!" I said, taking the gift. "Now I can read in bed after Lights Out. Thanks, Kristin!"

Diary, at the rate we're going, soon Mary-Kate and I will be as popular as Dana Woletsky. If only!

Anyway, I've got to keep this short and sweet. Phoebe just got a care package crammed with macadamia nut brownies. They look good, but I sure hope they're not vintage!

Dear Diary,

Sorry I didn't write yesterday but I was so busy and soooo psyched! Remember how worried I was that I'd be the worst student in my math class? Well, it turns out that I'm one of the best!

When my math teacher Mr. Geller found out how much I already learned back in Chicago, he told me I was off to an excellent start.

"How did you learn so much, Mary-Kate?" Mr. Geller asked as we were leaving the classroom.

Should I tell him about my tutor Taylor Donovan? And how he saved me from a lifetime of math phobia? Nah.

"I guess I've always had a passion for numbers," I said with a smile.

"Well, it certainly shows!" Mr. Geller said. "Keep up the good work, Mary-Kate."

I don't think I'll ever tell Mr. Geller about Taylor. Let him think I was born with a silver calculator in my mouth.

And speaking of numbers, you should hear all the girls who want us to help find them dates . . .

"There's a guy at Harrington who looks just like Ben Affleck," Alyssa Fuji said. "Can you fix him up with me?"

"What's his name?" I asked.

Alyssa shrugged. "No clue. Can't you find out?"

I thought I'd heard everything until Cheryl Miller came by. She waved her astrological chart in my face.

"My Sun-sign is Aquarius with my moon in Capricorn," Cheryl explained. "So it's important that I meet a boy who's either a Libra or a Gemini with Pisces rising."

"Oh, no problem!" I said.

The only girl who made sense was Campbell. She wanted a boy who was on the Harrington softball team. That way, they'd have something to talk about.

But even tracking down the softball team was hard. Especially when all the boys were complete strangers.

"Ashley, how are we going to find these guys when we don't even know what they look like?" I whispered to my sister in the school library.

Ashley shook her head. Then she stared over my shoulder and her eyes lit up. She pulled a book off the shelf and held it up.

"Ta-daaa! A Harrington School for Boys yearbook," Ashley said. She sat down next to me and opened it. "It's the most recent one. Are we lucky or what?"

I'll say! Ashley immediately flipped to the "L's"

and looked for Ross Lambert.

"There he is!" Ashley said. She slumped over the book and sighed. "No wonder he's a model."

I had to agree with Ashley. Ross looked as if he were right out of a Gap commercial. But what about P.J.?

I grabbed the book and flipped to the "J's". But then I stopped. "Hey, wait a minute," I said. "I have no idea what P.J.'s *real* name is."

"P.J. P.J.," Ashley repeated. She ran her finger along the page. Then she pointed to a guy with red hair and freckles. "Maybe it's Phillip Jacoby. He's cute."

"Or Peter Juarez!" I said, jabbing my finger at a dark-haired boy on the page. "What a babe!"

Mrs. Yancosek—the librarian—cleared her throat. She put her finger over her lips.

I quietly turned the page and looked for another P.J. There was one—Perry Joplin. It must have been a bad picture because he was staring into the camera with this surprised look on his face. And his shiny shirt with the wide lapels looked more like it belonged in Dad's yearbook!

"Could *that* be P.J.?" Ashley asked slowly.

I stared at the picture some more.

"I hope not," I said, shaking my head hard.

"Jeremy knows what I like."

"Then you'll find out who he is next Monday," Ashley said, shutting the book. "When the boys come over for lab."

"Oh, yeah!" I said.

I wondered who P.J. really was. Was he Phillip Jacoby? Peter Juarez? Perry Joplin? I wasn't sure whether I wanted to find out—or not!

*Who is P.J.?*

# Chapter 5

# Saturday

Dear Diary,

Do you believe it's Saturday? I never spent Saturday in school before. And I can't stop wondering what Jennifer and Nicole are doing today. The mall? The Cineplex? That was our usual Saturday drill.

Not that there aren't cool things to do here at White Oak. There are loads of clubs and activities to join. And Wendy told me that the school bus goes to the mall on weekends. (Could there be an extra bus for shopping bags?)

But today Saturday means only one thing—homework, homework, and more homework! Arrrgh!! So forgive the gross stain, Diary. When I'm exhausted, only chocolate chip cookies will do. You see, not only did Ms. Bloomberg give us more reading, but my other teachers piled on the homework, too. And all this on top of my *Oliver Twist* paper!!!

But homework isn't the only reason I'm so zonked-out. The Mary-Kate and Ashley Friendship Service is a huge success. So huge that just about everyone is asking us for help.

"You see?" I told Mary-Kate last night. "I told you it would work."

"Yeah, but I just wish we didn't have to make all of our calls in secret!" Mary-Kate complained. "I feel like a spy!"

Hey, gotta go, Diary. There's someone at the door. And either she wants a date for the dance or she's looking for a chocolate chip cookie. See ya!

Dear Diary,

Five days, six hours, and thirty minutes. My math must be pretty good because I just figured out how long Ashley and I have been here at White Oak.

So far so good—even though I do miss Dad and Carrie. I'm sure they miss Ashley and me, too—even though they're probably up to their elbows in "exotic" insects. Yuck! The things Dad does in the name of science.

Okay, you're probably wondering how the Mary-Kate and Ashley Friendship Service is holding up. Oh, *it's* holding up all right—but I am not!!

What was I *thinking*? Why did I tell Ashley I'd go along with this lame friendship service? Sure, it seemed like a pretty cool idea for a while, until *everybody* heard about it. I've been dialing our cell phone so much that I have a callus on my finger. So you can imagine how I felt when Ashley showed me her latest list of Harrington hopefuls.

"Ashley, this is dangerous," I whispered. We were doing our laundry in the Porter House laundry room. "Miss Viola is right outside talking to Lexy Martin."

"Miss Viola won't even hear us above the noise of the washing machines," Ashley said, snapping the cell phone open. Her voice changed. "Hello," she said into the phone. "This is Ashley Burke calling. Can you please find one of your house-mates for me? His name is—"

"Mary-Kate? Ashley?" a voice said. Our heads shot up. It was Miss Viola!

"Um," Ashley said into the phone. "His name is Kevin Burke. He's the one sorting the atlas moths from the tarantulas."

But Miss Viola didn't buy it. "You can hang up that phone now, Ashley," she said. "I doubt this is an emergency call to the Amazon."

Ashley sighed and clicked off the phone. We both stood up and faced Miss Viola.

"I'm a bit disappointed in you," Miss Viola said.

"I thought you understood our no cell phone rule."

"But Miss Viola," Ashley protested. "The house phone is impossible to get to."

"There's a reason for that," Miss Viola said. "We don't want girls here spending all their time on the phone."

"Does that mean you're going to take ours away?" I asked Miss Viola.

"No," Miss Viola said. "You're both new to White Oak and to our rules. You can keep the cell phone as long as you use it only in emergencies. As your father has said."

We thanked Miss Viola and watched her leave the room. I could tell that Ashley was upset.

"We can't end our friendship service now," Ashley complained. "It was on such a roll!"

"Well, it just rolled off a cliff," I said. "Face it, Ashley. From now on the Mary-Kate and Ashley Friendship Service is history."

I couldn't admit it to Ashley, diary, but I am totally relieved. Now we have a real excuse for not running our friendship service anymore.

But will Ashley stop? I'm not so sure . . .

# Chapter 6

# Sunday

Dear Diary,

I didn't think it would happen, but it did. The Mary-Kate and Ashley Friendship Service is out of service.

I felt pretty bad at first, but let's face it, Diary, Mary-Kate and I still came out way ahead. We met loads of new kids and we both have dates.

*And* we're going to meet the guys in science lab tomorrow. Maybe Ross and I will share a microscope. How romantic!!!!

Dear Diary,

Call me a slug, but I did practically nothing the entire day. That's right. Zero. Zip. Zilch!

 There's no way Ashley and I can run our friendship service. So instead of spending hours on our cell phone, I spent a whole Sunday watching women's basketball on TV..

I think I was born to be a couch potato.

# Chapter 7

# Monday

Dear Diary,

I never really liked Mondays. But  then again, Mondays never meant science lab with the Harrington boys!

"I'm so excited about seeing Ross for the first time that I can hardly eat!" I told Mary-Kate in the dining hall. I glanced at her tray. "You must be excited, too. You hardly touched your breakfast."

Mary-Kate shook her head. "Just grossed out," she said. "Who eats maple oatmeal with stewed prunes?"

After breakfast Mary-Kate and I made our way to the lab. The first thing I noticed when I stepped into the classroom were the boys. They were leaning over a counter and staring at some pickled frog inside a jar.

 I didn't have to look for Ross. I recognized him right away from his picture. And he recognized me because when we walked toward our seats he came over.

"You must be Ashley," Ross said.

"You must be right!" I answered. I could feel my

heart skipping inside my chest. "Are you ready for the dance this Friday?"

"Definitely," Ross said. "I hope you're practicing your Two-Step."

"My what?" I asked.

"It's some western dance I saw on the Hoe-down Channel," Ross explained.

"I'll be lucky if I can remember how to do-si-do," I said and laughed.

"Hey, we'll be fine," Ross said. He gave a little wave. "See you around."

"See you."

Ross sat down and I'd thought I'd melt. He was even cuter than his picture *and* he was planning to dance with me. Most guys would rather eat worms than dance! Literally.

I was about to run over and tell Mary-Kate when Dana tapped me on the shoulder.

"Ashley?" she asked. "Will you be my lab partner?"

"Sure, I will, Dana," I answered happily.

*Amazing!* I thought. Ross Lambert is my date. Dana Woletsky is my lab partner.

Dana and I sat down behind a tall counter as our lab teacher Mrs. Quinones passed out beakers filled with a thick, gummy liquid. She showed us how we can make polymers (that's a kind of plastic) by blowing air into the liquid with straws.

"I heard that you're going to the dance with Ross," Dana said, tapping the side of her beaker.

"Yeah," I said. "Is that way cool or what?"

"No, it is not way cool," Dana said.

"Why not?" I asked. I bent over and blew into my straw.

"Because Ross is my boyfriend, that's why!" Dana said.

I almost sucked down my polymer. "Your boyfriend?" I whispered.

"As if you didn't know," Dana whispered back. "Listen, Ashley. I want you to tell Ross that you will *not* go to the dance with him!"

I was so shocked I didn't know what to say.

"And do it before Friday night," Dana warned. "Or I'll announce to everyone at the dance that you stole my boyfriend!"

I couldn't believe my ears. Dana was threatening to humiliate me in front of everyone—in front of Ross! And as if that wasn't bad enough, she added one last zinger:

"And," Dana said, narrowing her eyes, "I'll tell everyone to stay away from you. So you can forget about ever making friends at White Oak!"

I stared at Dana, horrified. I knew full well that she could do what she was saying.

"Dana," I said. "This is crazy! I—"

Mrs. Quinones stepped behind us. "Girls? Is there a problem?" she asked.

"There was, Mrs. Quinones," Dana said sweetly. "But I offered Ashley a solution."

We carried on with our experiment in silence.

I was so confused I didn't even notice when my polymer oozed over my beaker onto the floor. I mean, why would Ross agree to go to the dance with me if Dana was his girlfriend? It didn't make any sense. He seemed like such a nice guy.

I tried to catch his eye across the room, but he never looked up. And when the bell rang, he left with a bunch of friends.

So the whole day went by and I haven't broken off my date—yet.

Diary, if Carrie was here she'd know what to do. But Carrie is thousands of miles away climbing palm trees. What am I going to do?

Dear Diary,

Today was the day I finally got to meet P.J. So I guess you could say I was pretty psyched. Especially when I walked into the science lab and checked out the guys from Harrington. Was P.J. the one with the spikey hair and wire-rimmed glasses? Or the cute guy with the high-tops?

"Yo, Mary-Kate!" Jeremy yelled from across the classroom. "Meet P.J.!"

I spun around and gasped. Standing next to Jeremy was Perry Joplin—the guy in the disco shirt. But today he was wearing blue jeans with cuffs and a short-sleeved lavender bowling shirt with the words "Wilma's Lanes" stitched on the chest. And he was holding a pickled frog!

"H-hi, Perry," I stammered.

Perry grinned widely at me.

"I'll leave you two alone," Jeremy said. He gave Perry a light slap on the back.

Perry and I stood there grinning at each other. I had to say something before my face cracked.

"Jeremy tells me you won a trophy," I said. "What was it for? Basketball? Football?"

"Edgar Allan Poe!" Perry said happily.

Whoa. Not the answer I was expecting. "Excuse me?" I asked.

"I won it last year in school, for my oral interpretation of 'The

"The Raven" award

54

Raven'!" Perry said. "It's my favorite poem."

"Oh . . . really?" I said.

Perry nodded. "In fact, I'm composing music for 'The Raven' on my organ. You should hear it. It's very intense!"

I stood there for a minute, then realized it was my turn to talk.

"Um . . . I won a couple of trophies for softball," I said. "How do you like those Cubs?"

Perry wrinkled his nose and shook his head. "I'm not much for hockey."

Hockey? Was he serious?

"Perry," I said, trying to be polite. "The Cubs are a Chicago baseball team. You know, the one Sammy Sosa plays for."

Perry looked confused. "Sammy who?"

I bit my lip—hard! To me, not knowing Sammy Sosa was like not knowing my own name!

I spotted Jeremy on the other side of the lab. He was watching us and snickering.

"I'll catch you later, Perry," I said. "There's someone I have to talk to."

"Okay!" Perry said. "See you at the dance!"

I walked over to Jeremy and pulled him aside.

"So how do you like Perry?" Jeremy asked.

"Jeremy, what were you thinking?" I groaned.

"Perry and I have nothing in common. Zero! Zip! Zilch!"

"Hey, Perry's a great guy," Jeremy said. He laughed. "I thought he'd help you get off on the right foot at White Oak."

I narrowed my eyes. "So this whole thing is a joke," I said. "Thanks loads!"

After class when we were leaving the lab, Ashley ran over. She told me that Jeremy fixed her up with Dana Woletsky's boyfriend!

"You were right, Mary-Kate," Ashley sighed. "I should never have trusted the family jokester!"

"Yeah, I know," I said. "But now the joke is definitely on us!"

# Chapter 8

# Tuesday

Dear Diary,

Can't write tonight, Diary. Wendy is  having a pizza party in her room. If you're wondering if I broke the date with Ross yet, the answer is no. To tell you the truth, I have no idea what to do. Do I go to the dance with a cute boy and end up with no friends? Or give up the date and feel sorry for the rest of my life?

Maybe the answer will come to me while I'm eating a pepperoni pizza. See you!

Dear Diary,

Just got back from Wendy's pizza party and I am totally stuffed! So stuffed I can hardly write.

It's funny. When I left Chicago I thought I'd never see another pizza again. But here, every Tuesday night, Mrs. Prichard sends a pizza to a different room on each floor. (I guess it's to make up for all that oatmeal!) And everyone on the floor is invited to pig out!

This is one tradition I can get used to.

But parties at boarding school sure are different from the ones back home. Since everyone lives just a few doors away, no one has to be driven by their mom or dad. It's kind of like having a sleepover without the sleeping bags or toothbrushes!

Tonight it was Wendy's turn to get the pizzas. Even though I'm not on her floor she invited me anyway. Which is great because Ashley was there, too.

"Is . . . Dana coming to the party?" Ashley asked Wendy as we sat in a circle on the floor. I could tell she was worried and trying hard to act cool.

"Nope," Wendy said. She grabbed a pepperoni slice. "Dana is in Phipps, the other First Form house, remember?"

"Oh, right!" Ashley said, looking relieved.

"I hope you saved me some pepperoni with extra cheese!" a voice called out.

I looked up and saw Dana's friend, Kristin Lindquist, coming through the door.

"Mary-Kate!" Ashley whispered to me as Kristen sat down and grabbed a slice. "Dana sent a spy!"

I shook my head. My sister was definitely losing it. "Calm down, Ashley," I whispered back. "Kristin lives on your floor, right?"

Ashley nodded.

"Then she came for pizza," I explained calmly. "Not information."

The pizza party was a blast. We talked about everything from movies, to teachers, to the Tasmanian Flu that was sweeping through White Oak.

"Four Third Form girls in Winslow House already have it," Lexy Martin said. "Fever, chills, the works."

"Oh, no!" Wendy cried. "I borrowed a pencil from a Third Form girl in the dining hall yesterday. I might have even . . . chewed on the eraser!"

"Ewww!"

"I hope it doesn't hit our house," Alyssa Fugi shuddered. "Especially with the Sadie Hawkins Day Dance coming up."

There it was. The "S" word.

"I am soooo psyched for that dance," Lexy said. "It's going to be the best Sadie Hawkins Day ever!"

"Thanks to Mary-Kate and Ashley," Kristin said. She looked straight at me and my sister. "And now that we have our dates, how about you two?"

I gulped down a chunk of pizza. "Us?"

"Yes—you!" Kristin laughed. "Who are you going to the dance with?"

"Come on, tell us," Wendy begged, wiggling closer. "We're all dying to know."

Ashley and I glanced at each other. I knew my

sister didn't want to talk about Ross. And I didn't really want to talk about Perry. So it was time to change the subject . . .

"Did anyone know that pizza was invented in the 1400's?" I asked quickly.

"But they didn't deliver until the 1500's," Ashley joked. She looked around the room. "Ha. Ha."

Everyone stared at us.

"That was a joke," Ashley said.

"Cute," Kristin said. "Now back to the dance. Ashley, let's start with you. Who are you going with?"

Kristin was looking at Ashley with piercing eyes. Maybe Ashley was right. Maybe Kristin was a spy!

"Me?" Ashley squeaked.

Kristin sighed. She pretended to look around the room. "Is there another Ashley in the room? I don't think so!"

I eyeballed my sister. Would she spill the beans about Ross Lambert? But instead, she spilled her soda . . .

"Ugh!" Ashley cried as cream soda dribbled down her shirt. "I am such a klutz. This had better come out!"

I watched Ashley run out of the room. Good thinking. But what was my excuse?

"Now, who's your date, Mary-Kate?" Alyssa asked.

"I'll bet he's fine!" Lexy said excitedly. "After all, you *did* have first dibs!"

"Come on, Mary-Kate," Wendy teased. "Tell us. Or we won't stop bugging you!"

Did she say—*bug*?

Suddenly I had a brilliant idea . . .

"Okay, okay. My date is," I began to say. Then I squinted at a wall. "Hey, wait a minute. Is that a *spider*?"

Sheer panic! All of the girls dropped their slices and jumped up.

"A spider?" Kristin shrieked.

"In my room?" Wendy cried.

"It's crawling around some-where," I said. "But don't worry. It might not even be a spider. According to my dad's textbook, it looked more like an African dung beetle."

In just a few seconds the room was clear and I had all the pizza to myself.

Well, Diary, that solved *that* problem. But it doesn't solve my problem with Perry!

# Chapter 9

# Wednesday

Dear Diary,

Two whole days and I still haven't  broken off my date with Ross. And the Sadie Hawkins Day Dance is creeping up on me!

Having Dana in my face doesn't make it easier. Today in Spanish class she passed me a note. It said, DID YOU BREAK THE DATE YET????? She must have wanted to know pretty bad because she added five question marks.

"I couldn't get near a phone, Dana!" I told her after class. "The line was too long."

"What about your cell phone?" Dana asked.

I stuck my chin in the air. "Miss Viola told Mary-Kate and me never to use our cell phones again."

So there.

Dana let out a big sigh. "Then why don't you just jump the line to the phone?"

"Are you serious?" I asked. "I could never steal someone's place on line."

I thought I saw flames shooting from Dana's eyes as she glared at me hard.

"Why not?" she asked through her teeth. "You already stole my boyfriend."

"Dana—"

"You'd better call Ross soon, Ashley," Dana said. "Or your only friend here at White Oak will be your sister."

Dana spun on her heel and walked down the hall.

"Boy. Do I need Dad and Carrie now!" I muttered under my breath.

The truth is, Diary, I would use the cell phone to break off the date—this is definitely an emergency. But I still can't do it. Ross is the neatest guy I ever met. How can I break a date with a guy like that?

So here's my choice: no Ross—or no friends!

I can live without a boyfriend for now, but I can't live without friends—no way!

I guess that's my decision. I'll sneak a call to Ross and break the date. It won't be easy, but at least I won't have Dana Woletsky on my back anymore.

Whoops—I just remembered—my *Oliver Twist* report is due tomorrow. And if I don't write it right now, I'll have someone *else* on my back. Ms. Bloomberg!!

Dear Diary,

Just got back my first math quiz.  When Mr. Geller handed it back to me, I saw this gigantic "O" written in red on the top. My hands shook as I stared at the paper.

"Z-zero?" I stammered. "No way!"

"On the contrary," Mr. Geller said. "It's an 'O' for outstanding. You got all the answers right, Mary-Kate."

Outstanding? Me? I wanted to draw a happy face inside that big wonderful O. Wait until Taylor Donovan gets a load of this.

And guess what? Mr. Geller explained that you don't even get F's at White Oak. Instead you get an NH for "needs help."

"It's all part of the White Oak grading system," Mr. Geller said.

Fine with me. Not that I plan to get any NH's. Although there is something I need help with right now. Nope. It's not English. Or science. Or history. It's BOYS!

I know what you're thinking, Diary. If I don't want to go to the dance with Perry, why don't I just secretly pick up the cell phone, call him, and tell him.

Well, I did! Almost.

There I was with the cell phone in my hand ready to call Perry when it hit me. Maybe he's really looking forward to going to the dance with me. Maybe he doesn't realize we have nothing in common. The last thing I want to do is hurt his feelings. I mean, it's not his fault we have nothing to talk about!

Except now I'm back to square one. Did Sadie Hawkins have these problems? I don't think so!

Dear Diary,

So—I finished *Oliver Twist* again. It was hard enough re-reading the whole book along with Ms. Bloomberg's other assignments. But when it came time to write the report—I choked. And I had just one day to do it, too!

Back home I would have asked Dad or Carrie for help, but this isn't home. It's the White Oak Academy and I am on my own!

"Ms. Bloomberg wants a theme. A theme!" I groaned to myself. I was sitting on my bed surrounded by my notebooks and my paperback copy of *Oliver Twist*. "Whatever happened to plain old book reports?"

"Ashley?" Phoebe asked from behind her screen.

I felt myself blush. "Oh, was I talking out loud? Sorry. I'll put a lid on it."

"No!" Phoebe said. She peeked out from behind the screen and smiled. "I have an idea for a theme. For your English paper."

"You do?" I asked.

Phoebe's curls bounced as she nodded. "Why don't you compare Oliver to kids today?"

"But how?" I asked. "Oliver Twist lived more than one hundred and fifty years ago. Practically ancient history!"

Phoebe came out from behind her screen and smiled. "Kids weren't that different back then. I mean, look at Oliver. He missed his mother. He even had peer pressure."

"Oh," I said, nodding slowly. "Oh, yeah."

I suddenly knew where Phoebe was going with this. I missed my mom ever since she died three years ago. And now I missed my dad. And I had peer pressure too—Dana Woletsky!

"I guess Oliver *wasn't* that different from us," I said. "He even went to boarding school."

"But we don't eat gruel," Phoebe giggled. "Just oatmeal!"

I jumped off my bed and gave Phoebe a hug.

*Please, sir, may I have some more oatmeal?*

"Thanks, Phoebe," I said. "You just did me an awesome favor. I wish I could do a favor for you."

I sat back on my bed and tried to think of ways I

could repay Phoebe. I could lend her my clothes. Nah. The most vintage thing I have are my clogs. Last season.

I could take her to a movie. Nah. She likes foreign movies and I hate subtitles.

There must be something in this world I could do for Phoebe. Wait! I've got it!

"Phoebe?" I asked, sitting up. "How would you like me to sneak a call to the Harrington School?"

Phoebe looked over her glasses. "What for?"

"The Sadie Hawkins Day Dance is in two days," I said. "Is there any boy you'd like me to ask for you?"

Phoebe started pacing back and forth.

That was a dumb question, I thought. Phoebe is into books and poetry and foreign films. She has other things to do besides—

"There is!" Phoebe shouted dramatically.

"Who?" I asked her, jumping off my bed. "Who?"

"There's only one boy at Harrington who I like," Phoebe whispered. "He reads poetry. Wears vintage clothes. And even plays a classical instrument."

"There's a guy like that at Harrington?" I asked, wrinkling my nose.

"Yes," Phoebe said. "His name is Perry Joplin!"

"Perry Joplin?" I gasped. "You mean the guy in

the yearbook with the shiny jacket?"

"That's him," Phoebe sighed. "He's the only boy at Harrington who's just like me!"

Phoebe's smile turned into a frown. "But I can't ask him out," she said. "Because somebody beat me to him. Your sister, Mary-Kate."

I grinned from ear to ear. Mary-Kate finally had an out. All she had to do was pass P.J. on to Phoebe. And all I had to do was find Mary-Kate and tell her the good news.

"Guess what, Phoebe?" I asked. "You are about to ask Perry Joplin to the Sadie Hawkins Day Dance."

"Really?" Phoebe asked. "How?"

"Let's just say that one favor deserves another," I said with a smile.

"Great," Phoebe said. "Oh, and Ashley. Can you do me one more favor?"

"What?" I asked.

Phoebe brushed off the dresser with her palm.

"Can you quit using that strawberry glitter lotion?" she asked. "It's like living with Tinker Bell!"

"It's a deal," I said.

So here's the plan, Diary. First, I've got to find Mary-Kate and tell her the good news. Second, I'm going to finish my *Oliver Twist* report. And third, I'm going to sneak a call to Ross tomorrow and break off our date—once and for all!

Oh, yeah, and there's a fourth . . .

I'VE GOT TO FIND ANOTHER DATE—FAST!!

Dear Diary,

Boy, am I off the hook! Ashley told me that her roommate Phoebe has a crush on P.J. I guess there's somebody for everybody in this world!

Phoebe was in my room when I made the call. "Hi, P.J.," I said into the phone. "It's me, Mary-Kate."

"Mary-Kate!" P.J. gushed. "I was just practicing the tango for the Sadie Hawkins Day Dance."

"The tango?" I said. "But P.J., it's a square dance. You know, western stuff."

"I know!" P.J. said. "But there *are* cowboys in Argentina. They're called gauchos!"

I looked up at the ceiling and sighed.

I could see Phoebe from the corner of my eye. She wasn't jumping up and down or biting her nails. She was just eyeing me, real serious.

"Listen, P.J., there's something I want to discuss with you," I said. "When I invited you to the dance

I didn't know that we don't have all that much in common. I mean, I live for sports, and you live for the organ—and Edgar Allan Poe. So I don't think we should go to the dance together."

Dead silence. Uh-oh—Perry's feelings were hurt!

"You . . . don't?" P.J. gulped.

"No. But I have really great news, too," I added quickly. "Because there's someone here who's absolutely nuts about you. Her name is Phoebe Cahill."

"Hey, I know who Phoebe is," P.J. said. "She writes excellent poetry. And her clothes are kind of cool, too."

"Then you like her?" I asked.

"I guess so," P.J. answered.

I smiled at Phoebe. She smiled back.

"Cool!" I said to P.J. "I'll put her on the phone. Here she is."

Phoebe grabbed the phone. "I didn't know they

called you P.J." she said. I couldn't tell what P.J. said next but Phoebe threw back her head and laughed. Then she began to recite: "What's in a name? That which we call a rose by any other name would smell as sweet."

I blinked hard. I knew that was from *Romeo and Juliet*. I also knew that all that sappy talk was making me sick!

But, hey, it worked.

"It's a date," Phoebe said as she clicked off the phone. "P.J. is going to the dance with me."

"Congratulations," I said.

"But what about you?" Phoebe asked, concerned. "Which boy will you ask to the dance?"

Good question. Especially since I had no other classes with the boys this week.

"No problem," I answered. "I'll just sneak another phone call to the Harrington dorm and get another date."

But not tonight. There's a hockey game in the TV room that I must see. I'll call tomorrow after classes.

Hmm. I wonder if Peter Juarez is still available.

# Chapter 10

# Thursday

Dear Diary,

 This morning I made up my mind. I absolutely had to sneak a call to Ross to break off our date. It was now or never. Tomorrow was the Sadie Hawkins Dance—and Dana was breathing down my neck!

So I tried calling right before first period class. I thought Ross would still be in his room then. He was—but he couldn't talk.

"Sorry, I've got to run to the dining hall," Ross said. "I got up late and I'm starving. I'll call you later."

"This will just take a second," I started to say. But he had already hung up.

Serves me right for waiting till the last minute, I thought. I threw the phone into my backpack and ran off to English class.

"Did you talk to Ross?" Dana hissed when I walked in.

"Later," I whispered back. I was really tired. I had spent all night writing my *Oliver Twist* report.

Luckily, it was really good. So when Ms. Bloomberg asked me to read it to the class I was ready to go!

I picked up my report and walked to the front of the class. I stood before the chalkboard and cleared my throat. Then I began to read.

"*Oliver Twist* was written by Charles Dickens in eighteen—"

BRRRRRRRIIIIIIIIIIING!!!

I froze. I knew that ring anywhere. And it was coming from my backpack!

"Oh, my," Ms. Bloomberg said, glancing at the clock. "Is that the bell already?"

BRRRRRRRIIIIIIIIIIING!!!

My heart began to pound. I forgot to switch off my cell phone! Ross was probably calling me back.

"What *is* that?" Ms. Bloomberg asked.

I chewed my lip as I stared at Mary-Kate. My sister was rolling her eyes and shaking her head. There was only one thing I could do. I had to hang up on whoever was calling me!

"E-excuse, me, please," I stammered as I walked over to my desk. I unzipped the backpack and took out the phone. My finger trembled as I clicked it off.

I took a deep breath.

"Ashley?" Ms. Bloomberg asked. "Why did you bring a phone to class? Don't you know the rules?"

I opened my mouth to speak but nothing came out. So Mary-Kate jumped up and did it for me.

"Our dad gave it to us, Ms. Bloomberg," Mary-Kate said. "It's for emergencies."

"Was that your father just now?" Ms. Bloomberg asked.

"No," I admitted.

Ms. Bloomberg raised an eyebrow. "Well, then it wasn't an emergency, was it?"

"No," I said again. I could feel my face burning.

"I'm afraid you'll have to give me the phone. I'll have to tell Mrs. Prichard about this." Ms. Bloomberg sighed.

I handed the phone to Ms. Bloomberg.

"Now, Ashley, will you please continue with your report?"

I opened my mouth to speak—and the phone rang again!

Mrs. Bloomberg answered it. "Hello?" she said. "No, I'm afraid she can't come to the phone right now. Whom shall I say is calling? Ross? I'll let her know."

I glanced over at Dana. Her face was bright red—and she was glaring right at me!

I wanted to sink through the floor.

74

And I still had to get through the rest of my report.

By then I was so embarrassed I might as well have been reading the phone book. What will happen to Mary-Kate and me when Mrs. Prichard finds out? Will she suspend us? And if so, where will we go? To the Amazon?

I sneaked a peek at Dana again. She was still fuming.

On the other hand, the Amazon might be a pretty good idea right now.

Dear Diary,

Mrs. Prichard called us in after lunch. I could hear my heart pounding as Ashley and I sat in her office. What would she do to us?

"You girls have broken a very important White Oak rule," Mrs. Prichard said. "One which Miss Viola has already told you about. Twice. Am I right?"

"Yes, Mrs. Prichard," was all we could say.

"Then I'm afraid I'll have to confiscate your phone, girls," Mrs. Prichard said.

Confiscate. I knew that word. Back in Chicago I had teachers confiscate comic books, candy, even a pet salamander. Confiscating our cell phone wasn't so bad.

"I'm also taking away *all* of your telephone privileges for a month," Mrs. Prichard said. "That includes all house phones."

Ashley looked panicked. "But what if there's a real emergency?" she asked Mrs. Prichard. "Like Dad said?"

Mrs. Prichard gave us a small smile. "If it's an emergency you'll need to get permission to use the phone."

I was hoping Mrs. Prichard was finished.

No such luck.

"And there will be no evening activities for a week," Mrs. Prichard went on. "No TV. No pizza parties."

Did that include the Sadie Hawkins Day Dance? I wasn't sure.

Hey, wait a minute. Not going to the dance wouldn't be so bad. It would save me the trouble of finding another date and Ashley the trouble of breaking her date with Ross!

"Mrs. Prichard?" I asked slowly. "Does that mean we can't go to the Sadie Hawkins Day Dance?"

From the corner of my eye I saw Ashley straightening up in her seat. Was she thinking what I was thinking?

"I gave the dance a lot of thought," Mrs. Prichard

sighed. "And yes, you *can* go."

"W-we can?" Ashley asked.

Mrs. Prichard nodded. "Your dates from Harrington shouldn't have to suffer because of your punishment."

Ashley slumped down in her seat again. Rats!

"It's a shame you two had to start your first month at White Oak on the wrong foot," Mrs. Prichard said. "And I'm sure your father will be disappointed."

*Two left feet*

Dad? I stared at Ashley. She looked pretty worried, too.

"Are you going to tell our father, Mrs. Prichard?" Ashley asked.

"Please don't," I said.

"I won't have to, girls," Mrs. Prichard said. "Your phone bill is probably on its way to South America right now."

The phone bill—I forgot about that!

My only hope is that the mail will never reach Dad. I mean, maybe the Amazon rain forest is too thick for mail carriers to get through. And maybe by the time they force their way in, the mail will be too wet to read. Or better yet—maybe there is no mail delivery in the Amazon!

My head was spinning with possibilities when Mrs. Prichard held out her hand.

"Now, then," Mrs. Prichard said. "Give me the phone and I'll take good care of it."

Ashley handed it over and Mrs. Prichard dropped the phone in her desk drawer and slammed it shut. "You may go now," was all she said.

Ashley and I left Mrs. Prichard's office. As soon as we were in the hall, we turned to each other.

"What are we going to do without our cell phone, Mary-Kate?" Ashley cried.

I shook my head. "We're going to deal with it," I said. "I'm going to the dance without a date, and you're going with Ross Lambert."

"But I can't go with Ross," Ashley cried. "Dana will kill me!"

"Get real, Ashley," I said. "If Dana is the coolest girl at White Oak, she probably has dozens of other guys already lined up. And if Ross were so crazy about her, he'd be Dana's date in the first place!"

"You think?" Ashley asked slowly.

"Sure," I said. I tried to sound more certain than I felt.

We put on our coats and scarves and walked out of the Main Building. The icy February wind whipped our faces as we hurried to our house.

As we neared Porter House, Ashley turned to me. "Maybe you're right, and Dana will find another date for the dance," she said. "But she's still going to announce that I stole her boyfriend.

"After tomorrow night, I might be the only girl at White Oak without any friends!"

# Friday

Dear Diary,

I almost couldn't get to sleep last night, I was so worried about Dana. But when I woke up this morning I decided to concentrate on the dance. If this was going to be the last night of my life, at least I would be prepared for it!

Including being well-dressed. I decided to wear my short-sleeved powder blue shift with my black patent leather sling-back shoes.

"Very swank," Phoebe said.

You should have seen *Phoebe's* outfit—a light green chiffon dress with matching high-heeled pumps. Vintage, of course. I knew she had a petticoat underneath because it crunched every time she sat down. Her curly hair was blown-out and styled in a flip. She even had a tiny dark green velvet bow clipped on the side.

"Well?" Phoebe asked me, twirling around in our room. "What do you think?"

"Very . . . vintage!" I said with a smile.

"Thanks!" Phoebe said cheerily.

## Calling All Boys

Getting dressed was fun and it took my mind off my real worry. Coming face to face with Dana Woletsky!!

What would Dana say when she saw me at the dance with Ross? And worse—what would she do? Would she carry out her threat and make me friendless in New Hampshire?

Mary-Kate had headed off to the dance early, so Phoebe and I walked out together. We ran into Wendy on the main path leading to the gym. The path was filled with kids. I looked around. Was one of them Dana?

"Hey, you guys. Let's not walk on the path!" I suggested. "Let's take the long way!"

Wendy and Phoebe looked at me as if I were from Mars.

"You mean across the field?" Phoebe complained. "But it's covered with snow and slush!"

"And no way are we wearing rubber boots tonight," Wendy said. She lifted her foot to show her black patent leather platform shoe.

"Oh, come on. It'll be fun," I said. "How often do we get to walk through the snow—under the stars?"

Phoebe's eyes lit up. "When you put it that way, it does sound

81

awfully romantic," she said. "Let's do it, Wendy."

"Oh, all right," Wendy groaned under her breath. But she came with us as we skipped over slush puddles and climbed over snow. And Dana Woletsky was nowhere in sight.

"This dance is going to be a blast!" Wendy said as we neared the gym. "And I can get used to asking boys out."

"Definitely," Phoebe said, stomping snow off of her pumps. "If you ask me, Sadie Hawkins was a real crusader for women's rights. Wouldn't you agree, Ashley?"

"Sure," I said. But I really wasn't paying too much attention. I was still too busy worrying about Dana.

Maybe Mary-Kate is right, I thought. Dana must know by now that I didn't break off my date with Ross. So she must have found another boy to ask to the dance. And maybe she'll like him so much she'll forget all about being mad at me. Maybe.

Once inside, Phoebe, Wendy, and I hung up our coats in the foyer. I glanced around for Dana. I knew I would run into her sooner or later. Hopefully later. Much, *much* later!

"Hi, Ashley," a boy's voice said.

I spun around. It was Ross, looking very dressed

up in tan pants and a navy blue blazer.

"Hi, Ross!" I said, my mouth dropping open. He looked C-U-T-E! So cute that for a moment I forgot all about Dana!

"Want to go inside?" Ross asked. He pointed to the gym a bit nervously. "The band started play-ing."

"Sure," I answered. If my old friends Jennifer and Nicole could see me now!

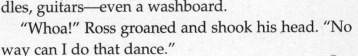

Ross and I walked into the gym. Some kids were already dancing in two long lines to a country band. They played fid-dles, guitars—even a washboard.

"Whoa!" Ross groaned and shook his head. "No way can I do that dance."

"Oh, yes, you can!" I teased. I grabbed a plastic cowboy hat from a table and plopped it on Ross's head. "Just think of it as the electric slide with cow-boy hats."

We fell into line and copied what everyone else was doing. I wanted to dance with Ross all night. Until I spotted a girl who looked like Dana.

And that jolted me back to reality. What was I doing? Was I really at a square dance with someone else's boyfriend?

"Ashley, what's up?" Ross yelled over the music.

My mouth felt dry. How could I tell Ross the truth? Then again, how could I *not*?

"Uh, Ross," I said, "Dana Woletsky told me something about you last week. And I kind of thought it wasn't true—but now I'm kind of worried that it was—"

"Don't tell me, let me guess," Ross said. He began to snicker. "She told you about the time I put bubble gum on her seat in first grade?"

I wrinkled my nose. "No."

"Then she told you about the time she was running for third grade class president," Ross said. "And I drew a mustache and horns on her campaign poster?"

Bubble gum? Mustache and horns? This guy was worse than Jeremy!

"No, no," I said. "Dana told me that she had a boyfriend at Harrington. And that boy was you."

There. I said it. And it felt a lot better once it was out. Sort of like a splinter.

Ross stared at me. Then he laughed so hard I could see the fillings in his teeth. "Give me a break!" he shouted. "Dana isn't my girlfriend. I'm her *friend*, that's all. And knowing Dana, I'm sure she found someone else to ask to the dance."

I felt a smile slowly spreading across my face. "Really?" I asked.

"Really," he said, flashing me an incredible smile.

I was so happy I wanted to give Ross a huge hug. But it *was* our first date.

We were having a great time. And Ross was such a gentleman. He even went to the snack table to get us both punch. That's when Kristin Lindquist came over looking very serious.

"Don't think you're off the hook, Ashley," Kristin said. She folded her arms across her chest. "Because you're not."

"Off the hook?" I asked, surprised. "What are you talking about, Kristin?"

"Lucky for you Dana couldn't come to the dance," Kristin said. "She's in bed with the Tasmanian Flu."

The flu! So that explained why I hadn't seen Dana all night.

"How is Dana?" I asked. "Does she have a fever?"

"As if you care," Kristen snorted. "You didn't care when you went to the dance with Dana's boyfriend. She told me she's never going to forget it and I don't blame her!"

Kristen flipped her hair over her shoulder and turned around. Then she began to walk away.

"Kristen, wait!" I called.

I wanted to tell Kristin what Ross told me. That he and Dana were just friends. But what difference would it make? Dana is going to get me back—no matter what the truth is!

As I watched Ross come over with two cups of strawberry punch I felt sick. *Real* sick.

And it wasn't the Tasmanian Flu!

Dear Diary,

Well, I found out what all dateless  girls do at the Sadie Hawkins Day Dance. They serve refreshments! Another White Oak tradition, I guess.

My adventures in chips-and-dip began at six-thirty sharp. That's when I reported for duty. I was glad to see I had company. Three other girls—one from Second Form, one from Fourth, and even one from First—Alyssa! Her dream date came down with the Tasmanian Flu.

While we waited for Mrs. Prichard to come and give us the drill, we watched the Fifth and Sixth Form girls put the last touches on the decorations: cardboard barn animals, crepe paper, and signs with sayings like "Yee-ha!" "Do-si-do!" And "Rope dem Doggies." Corny—but fun.

# Calling All Boys

"Well!" Mrs. Prichard said when she saw us. "How are my little Sadie Ladies?"

Sadie Ladies? I guess that's another name for the Dateless Four.

"Now, then," Mrs. Prichard said. She reached into a shopping bag. "Since this is a square dance, I'd like you all to dress accordingly."

I stared as Mrs. Prichard handed out plastic cowboy hats and red bandannas. I rolled my eyes. How cute.

Then Mrs. Prichard peered through her glasses at a clipboard. "We need one person to be in charge of the punch bowl, another to stack paper plates and cups, one to supervise the chips and dips and last but not least, someone to line up the soda bottles and other beverages."

"I'll do that, Mrs. Prichard," I volunteered. I had lots of practice lugging soda bottles up to our attic in Chicago!

I rolled up my sleeves and got to work. In fact, I really got into it. I had all the bottles lined up on the table according to flavor. Cola, orange, grape, cream soda. I was about to tackle the chocolate milk when I felt someone tap my shoulder.

"Excuse me," a boy's voice said.

Holding a container of milk, I glanced over my

shoulder. A boy with black hair and black eyes was standing behind me. He still had his jacket on.

"Is this the snack table?" he asked.

"It is," I explained. "But we're not ready yet."

"That's okay," he said. "I'm here to help out."

Help out? I guess that Harrington had the same tradition as White Oak!

"My name is Grant Marino," the boy said. "I'm new at Harrington."

I couldn't believe it. Grant was adorable—how did Ashley and I miss him?

"Hi," I told Grant. "Why don't you hang up your jacket and start opening cracker boxes?"

"Gotcha," Grant said. He began taking off his jacket. That's when I flipped. Underneath Grant's jacket was a navy blue Cubs sweatshirt!

"You like the Cubs?" I asked.

Grant gave a thumbs-up sign. "Sammy rules!"

I plunked my container on the table. "I'm a Cubs fan too," I said. "Probably because I'm from Chicago."

"Chicago? No kidding!" Grant said. "So am I. Well, right outside the city anyway."

Not only was Grant from Chicago but he also hung out at some of my favorite places—the Windy City Laser Arcade, the City Cineplex and even the Super Scooper!

"My favorite sundae is Freaky Fudge," Grant said.

"Mine too!" I cried. "With three scoops and extra sprinkles!"

Then it occurred to me. Grant didn't have a date. And neither did I.

"Hey, Grant?" I asked, tilting my head. "How would you like to go to the dance?"

"We are at the dance," Grant said with a shrug.

"No, no!" I laughed. "I mean go to the dance with me. It is Sadie Hawkins Day, you know."

"You mean—a date?" Grant asked, his voice cracking.

"I think that's what they call it," I joked.

"Sure, thanks," Grant said, blushing a bit. "But what about the snack table?"

I grabbed the cracker boxes and put them next to the guacamole.

"Job's done!" I said. I whipped off my goofy hat and smiled. "Now let's party on!"

We squeezed through a crowd of kids. I was about to look for Ashley when I spotted someone I knew on the dance floor. It was Phoebe Cahill, and she was dancing with this really cute guy. My eyes popped wide open as I looked closer—the cute guy was Perry Joplin!

I hardly recognized Perry without his bowling shirt and vintage jeans. This time he was wearing a white tuxedo with a red carnation stuck in the lapel. His dark hair was slicked back and on his feet were black snakeskin cowboy boots. Pretty sharp!

And Diary, you should have seen them dance. They looked as if they'd been practicing for years!

Okay, I guess I judged Perry a little too quickly. I mean, he may not know much about the Cubs but he is real smart and he sure can dance!

And you know what—so can I! "Let's dance!" I told Grant.

He pointed to Perry and Phoebe. "You mean—like that?"

"We can try," I said.

Soon Grant and I were square dancing side-by-side with Perry and Phoebe. And having a blast!

When I finally spotted Ashley I could see she was having a great time with Ross. Especially since Dana Woletsky was nowhere in sight!

Diary, all I can say is this: Sadie Hawkins sure knows how to throw a dance. Yeee-haaaa!

# Chapter 12

# Saturday

Dear Diary,

Last night I had the most fabulous  dream! I dreamt I was at the movies, sitting next to Ross and sharing a box of buttered popcorn. Then suddenly Ross spilled his popcorn all over the floor and—are you ready?—the kernels formed this huge heart with our initials inside. And if that wasn't enough, the kernels were still popping—just like butter-coated fireworks!

But the problem with awesome dreams is that you wake up just as they're really getting good. And that's when you have to face reality. Or in my case, Dana Woletsky!

Mary-Kate couldn't stop talking about the dance. "Was that the coolest dance or what?" she kept saying.

"Way cool," I said. I gave my sister a little nudge. "And I saw you dancing with the Cubs fan."

"Oh, yeah," Mary-Kate said, blushing a little. She plunked a blueberry muffin on her tray.

"Mary-Kate," I said, glancing around the dining

room. "I have to tell you something. It's about Dana."

"Don't bother," Mary-Kate said. She grinned and grabbed a bowl of oatmeal. "I know Dana wasn't at the dance last night. Are you lucky or what?"

"Not exactly," I said slowly. "I heard from Kristin that Dana is still mad that I went to the dance with Ross. Even though Ross told me they were just friends."

Mary-Kate put a bowl of oatmeal on my tray. "Forget about it, Ashley," she sighed.

"Forget about it? How can I?" I said. "Dana has a score to settle. And that score is me!"

My sister looked me square in the eye. "Dana also has the Tasmanian Flu," she said. "Which means she'll be sneezing her brains out in bed for at least another week!"

I thought about it and began to relax.

"You're right," I said. "Dana is probably so loaded with aspirins now that the last thing on her mind is me. Or the Sadie Hawkins Day Dance."

"Now you're talking!" Mary-Kate said.

I smiled as I placed a blueberry muffin on my tray. "And you know what, Mary-Kate?" I asked. "I think we're really going to like it here at White Oak. Our first two weeks have gone pretty well."

"Well," Mary-Kate said, "if you don't count having our cell phone taken away. Or being grounded. Or eating oatmeal for breakfast every day."

"Or Ms. Bloomberg!" I added, making a face. "But look at all the good things. We both have roommates we like. We got to meet boys. And we're already on our way to making new friends—"

"—AHHHH-CHOOOO!!"

We were interrupted by the biggest sneeze I ever heard. And I had a not-so-funny feeling I knew whose sneeze it was.

"Dana?" I whispered to myself.

No. It couldn't be. I leaned over and glanced down the breakfast line. Sure enough, there she was. Looking sick in a bathrobe and clutching a soggy tissue in her fist.

"Mary-Kate, she's here!" I cried. "Dana's here!"

"Okay, girls!" Mrs. Weinstock, the dining hall lady, called from behind the counter. "Keep it moving!"

Mary-Kate and I slid our trays along the metal ledge. There was no avoiding it. We were going to have to pass Dana on our way to the table.

"Um, h-hi, Dana," I stammered, trying to be nice.

Dana was facing a shelf filled with mugs of hot

tea so I couldn't see her face. But I did see her arms tense and her shoulders hunch up.

*friendly gargoyle*

I watched as Dana clunked a mug on her tray. Then she turned around slowly, real slowly—and her face—well, let's just say that the gargoyles looked a lot friendlier that morning!

"Don't think it's over, Ashley," Dana said through a stuffed nose and clenched teeth. "Because it's *not*!"

I wanted to speak but Mary-Kate tugged at my arm.

"Feel better, Dana," Mary-Kate said cheerily. "And get lots of rest!"

As I quickly followed my sister past the portraits of the ex-headmistresses to an empty table, I knew I had spoken too soon. Way too soon.

"You know what, Mary-Kate?" I said. My chair scraped against the floor as I sat down.

"No, what?" Mary-Kate asked.

I slumped over my hot oatmeal with sliced bananas and sighed. "Fitting in at the White Oak Academy is not going to be as easy as I thought."

My sister dug her spoon into her steaming hot oatmeal and stirred it around. "No one said it was going to be easy, Ashley," Mary-Kate said. She gave a small smile. "But I do think it's going to be fun."

Diary, I looked around at all the girls in the dining hall. At the stone gargoyles and at the snow falling outside the big, tall windows. And I knew that Mary-Kate was right! Mary-Kate and I were having a great time at White Oak.

And it was just going to get better!

Way
to go,
White
Oak!

PSST! Take a sneak peek
at

# TWO of a kind™
## Diaries

## #10 Winner Take All

Dear Diary,

Today was one of the most embar-
rassing days of my entire life. I totally
choked at softball tryouts!

I have no clue what happened. Maybe I was trying too hard to make Coach Salvatore notice me.
After all, I do want to make the White Oak softball
team more than anything else in the world. I just *had*
to show her what a great player I was.

Well, Coach noticed me all right. Because I was
the worst player on the field!

First, I blew an easy out at third. Then I dropped
a fly ball. Finally I struck out—five times!

"Hey Mary-Kate, what's the matter?" My roommate Campbell jogged up to me. "You were much
better at practice."

"Beats me," I said with a sigh. "I guess I'm having an off day. Way off."

Campbell hesitated. "Uh, Mary-Kate, about that team you play for at home—the Bashers? What kind of record did you guys have last season?"

That made me mad. The Bashers were great! "We practically won the championship last year!" I said. "And I bet we—I mean they—*do* win it this year."

Only they'll have to win it without me. I keep forgetting I'm not a Basher anymore. And if things keep going this way, I'm not going to be a Mighty Oak, either.

Something tells me I'm going to miss being on my hometown softball team this year. Oh, why can't they move White Oak Academy to Chicago?

Dear Diary,

Well, I guess my interview at the White Oak newspaper went better than Mary-Kate's softball tryout. It was a little rough at first, though.

At three o'clock on the dot I walked over to the *Acorn* staff room. I was supposed to talk to the Special Features Editor, whoever that was. Someone motioned me into a smaller room. I peeked in and whom did I see—but Dana Woletsky!

My mouth dropped open. Dana was the last person I expected! I knew she was still mad at me about asking Ross to the Sadie Hawkins Day Dance. If *she* was the Special Features Editor, she'd never give me a job at the newspaper.

Dana looked up and gave me a real sour look. "I was so *not* excited when Ms. Bloomberg told me I had to find a place for you on the staff," she said. "But I had to tell her we do need another writer." She leaned forward over her desk. "I have a job for you if you want it."

"You do?" I was so excited my voice squeaked. "Doing what?"

"I think you'd be perfect as"—Dana paused — "the new *Acorn* gossip columnist."

A gossip columnist! I was so surprised I didn't know what to think. Gossip columnists had to find out stuff nobody wanted them to know. That could be fun. Or it could get me into trouble.

On the other hand, being a gossip columnist would be a perfect way to find out what was really going on at White Oak. This way, I could get the scoop on what was in, what was out—and all the best parties! I was starting to like this idea.

"Well, what do you say?" Dana asked.

I took a deep breath. "Okay," I said. "I'll do it."

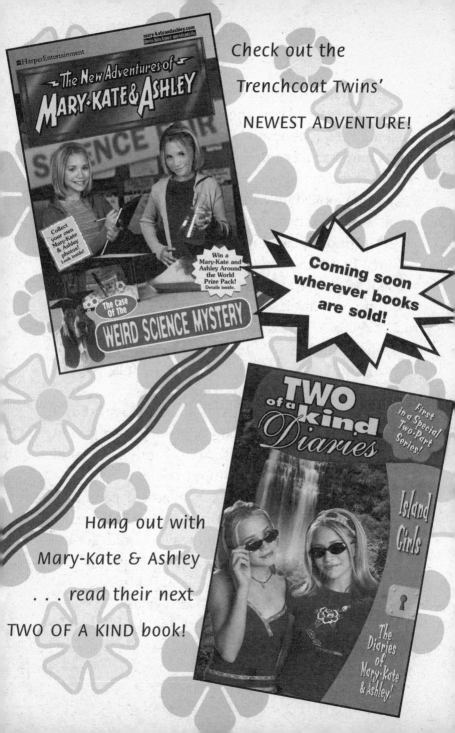

The Countdown to

# MARY-KATE AND ASHLEY'S

## BEST BIRTHDAY EVER BEGINS!

BOOK 1

Mary-Kate and Ashley

# Sweet 16

Never Been Kissed

Win a birthday party and phone call from Mary-Kate and Ashley

mary-kateandashley.com
America Online Keyword: mary-kateandashley

"The first book in a 3 Book miniseries—On Sale in April!"

mary-kateandashley.com
America Online Keyword: mary-kateandashley

 DUALSTAR PUBLICATIONS

 Books for Real Girls

HarperEntertainment
*An Imprint of HarperCollinsPublishers*
www.harpercollins.com

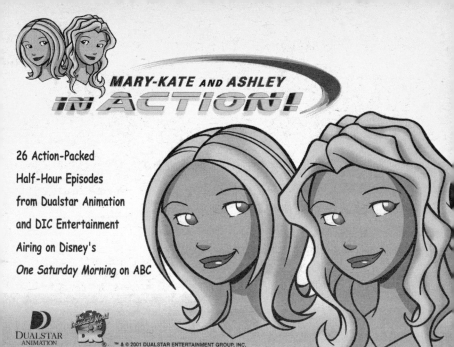

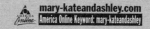

# Reading Checklist

**and ashley**

## single one!

☐ It's a Twin Thing

☐ How to Flunk Your First Date

☐ The Sleepover Secret

☐ One Twin Too Many

☐ To Snoop or Not to Snoop?

☐ My Sister the Supermodel

☐ Two's a Crowd

☐ Let's Party!

☐ Calling All Boys

☐ Winner Take All

☐ P. S. Wish You Were Here

☐ The Cool Club

☐ War of the Wardrobes

☐ Bye-Bye Boyfriend

☐ It's Snow Problem

☐ Likes Me, Likes Me Not

☐ Shore Thing

☐ Two for the Road

☐ Surprise, Surprise

☐ Sealed With a Kiss

☐ Now You See Him, Now you Don't

### Super Specials:

☐ My Mary-Kate & Ashley Diary

☐ Our Story

☐ Passport to Paris Scrapbook

☐ Be My Valentine

**Available wherever books are sold,
or call 1-800-331-3761 to order.**

# LOG ON!

**mary-kateandashley.com**
America Online Keyword: mary-kateandashley

**DUALSTAR ONLINE**

Real Talk for Real Girls

## Do you have all the Mary-Kate and Ashley books?

## Turn the page to find out!